Wear your
crown
proudly!

Darryianne
Brown

For my late grandparents, Grandfather Darryl "Dukey" Brown and Great-Grandmother Annie Mae Brown.

MAY YOU CONTINUE TO BE MY INSPIRATION.

www.mascotbooks.com

Aida Brown's Big Sister Crown

©2018 Damyionne Brown. All Rights Reserved. No part of this publication may be reproduced, stored in a retrieval system or transmitted in any form by any means electronic, mechanical, or photocopying, recording or otherwise without the permission of the author.

For more information, please contact:
Mascot Books
620 Herndon Parkway, Suite 320
Herndon, VA 20170
info@mascotbooks.com

Library of Congress Control Number: 2017915637

CPSIA Code: PRT1217A
ISBN-13:978-1-68401-544-3

Printed in the United States

AIDA BROWN'S
Big Sister CROWN

Written by
Damyionne Brown
Co-authored by
Damian Brown Sr.

Illustrated by
Yasushi Matsuoka

"**Good morning, Aida**. Did you sleep well, princess?"

"Good morning, Daddy. Yes, I did! Will I become a big sister today?" asked Aida.

Aida's dad smiled. "Well sweetheart, it depends if your mother goes into labor."

"Labor? What's labor?" asked Aida.

"Labor is when a woman shows signs that it's time to have her baby," said Aida's dad.

"**WOW!**" said Aida. "I want to see if Mommy is showing signs. I want to be a big sister soon!"

And off Aida went to her mother's bedroom.

"Mommy! Mommy!"

Aida shouted. "You have to show me a sign! A sign that tells me I'm going to be a big sister soon!"

Aida's mom laughed. "It's not time yet baby, but don't worry, I'll make sure you're the first to know when it is. Now, how about some breakfast?"

Aida's mom kissed Aida on the forehead, then they both headed downstairs for breakfast.

Once breakfast was made, everyone sat together at the table to eat.

"What are some things you'd like to teach the baby, Aida?" Aida's dad asked.

"Well," said Aida. "I can teach the baby how to **color**, give **big hugs**, and how to **make new friends**. Will the baby have a very special crown like my friends and me?"

"Yes, dear. Remember, we're all special in our own way," said Aida's mom. "The baby will be its own little person and have something special about him or her."

"You're going to be a **terrific** big sister, my sweet girl!" said Aida's dad. "Can I have one of those big hugs?"

"Sure, Daddy!" laughed Aida, then she jumped right into her dad's lap.

After breakfast, Aida colored a picture of her favorite jungle animals. She was just finishing the lion's mane when suddenly, she heard a shout.

"Honey! Aida!"

"Oh dear," said Aida's dad. "That's Mommy. She may be getting close."

"Was that a sign?" asked Aida.

"Hop on my back and let's go find out!" said Aida's dad.

"We're coming, Mommy!" cried Aida.

Aida's mom was sitting at the table breathing deep breaths.

"Was that the sign, Mommy?" asked Aida, her eyes lighting up.

Aida's mom inhaled slowly, then exhaled. "Aida sweetheart, I think it was. Mommy's going into labor. Will you help me prepare for the new baby? Go and find your Grandmother Annie. Daddy will stay here with me."

"Yes, Mommy," said Aida.

As Aida went to find her grandmother, she thought about becoming a big sister.

Was being a big sister *hard?* Would she have to share all her things? She was so used to having her own toys, crayons, and friends, but now she'd have to share them all. She wasn't going to be the baby anymore either. Would that mean she'd even have to *share her parents?*

Aida was worrying so much, she nearly ran right into her grandmother.

"What's wrong, Aida? What's wrong?" asked Aida's grandmother.

"I don't want to be a big sister!" cried Aida. "But Mommy showed the sign and now I'm going to be!"

"Why not?" asked her grandmother. "I just know you'll be the best big sister. Why are you worried?"

"Because..." Aida started, holding back tears. "Because I won't be the baby anymore, Mommy and Daddy will have a new baby, and I'm going to have to share them."

"Sweetheart," said Aida's grandmother, "being a big sister is very important. Only a super girl like you can do it. I know it'll be new and it'll be challenging at times, but Mommy and Daddy will need your help. Do you think you can do it?

Aida thought hard. "I think so."

"Wonderful!" said Aida's grandmother. "Now let's go get ready to welcome the baby!"

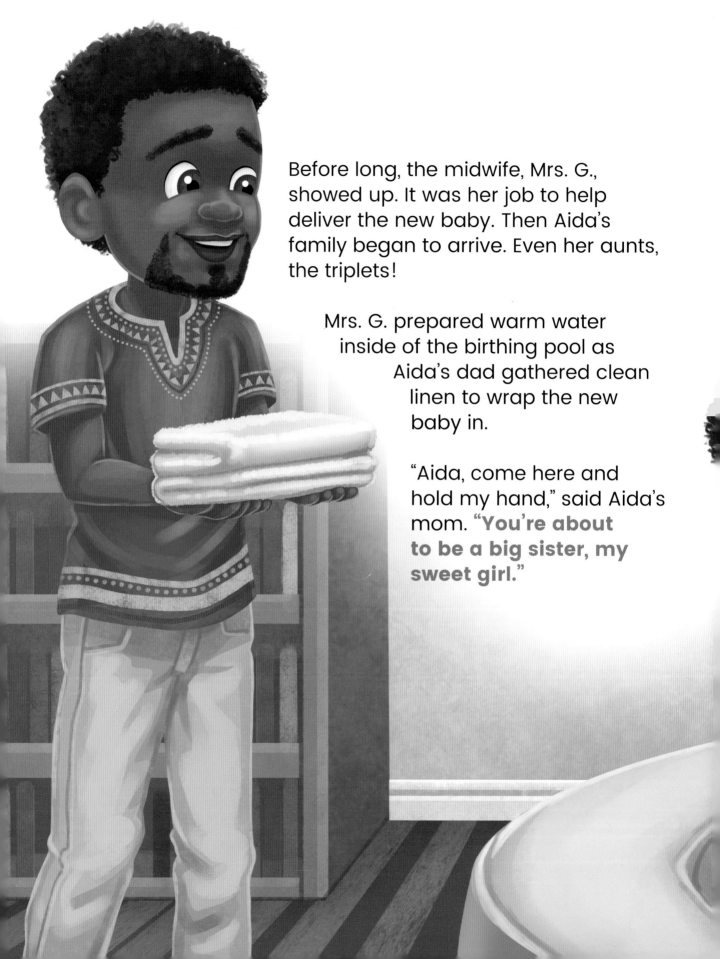

Before long, the midwife, Mrs. G., showed up. It was her job to help deliver the new baby. Then Aida's family began to arrive. Even her aunts, the triplets!

Mrs. G. prepared warm water inside of the birthing pool as Aida's dad gathered clean linen to wrap the new baby in.

"Aida, come here and hold my hand," said Aida's mom. "You're about to be a big sister, my sweet girl."

"Linen cloths, please!" shouted Mrs. G. *"It's a boy! It's a boy!"*

Everyone cheered and clapped.

Mrs. G. wrapped the new baby boy in a cloth, then laid him on his mother's chest. Aida's mom gazed into her new baby boy's brown eyes, touched his soft skin, and she began to cry tears of joy.

"Time to meet your big sister," she said to the baby. "Aida, would you like to meet your new baby brother?"

Aida ran over swiftly and reached out to her new little brother. He was perfect. "What are we going to call him?" asked Aida.

"Aidan Darryl Brown," said Aida's mom. "But we'll call him Dukey."

After a day of celebration, Aida's mom needed her rest, so the family began to leave. Aida's dad helped Aida, her mom, and little Aidan prepare for bed.

He ran Aida a bath with bubble gum-scented bubbles. Then Aida brushed her teeth and put on her pajamas. As she dozed off to her favorite bedtime story, Aida suddenly remembered something.

"I forgot to tell Aidan goodnight!"

Aida left her bed and headed to Aidan's crib as quietly as she could.

On her tippy toes, she leaned over Aidan's crib and said, "Goodnight, baby brother. I promise to be the best big sister ever. I love you!"

Aida went back to her room and dreamt of all of the fun things she and baby Aidan would play together.

Aida learned that becoming a big sister wasn't so bad after all. She now knows that her parents will always love her and understands that her little brother will need her help.

The End!

ABOUT THE AUTHOR

Originally from New Orleans, Louisiana, Damyionne Brown grew up with aspirations of being a school teacher and an author. When her childhood changed dramatically after her family was displaced by Hurricane Katrina, Damyionne never lost sight of her dreams. Having also worn afro puffs similar to Aida's, it gave her the inspiration to create the character that would star in her first children's book, *Aida Brown Finds Her Crown*.

Today she teaches first grade in Baton Rouge, Louisiana, and *Aida Brown's Big Sister Crown* is the second book in *The Book of Aida Series*!